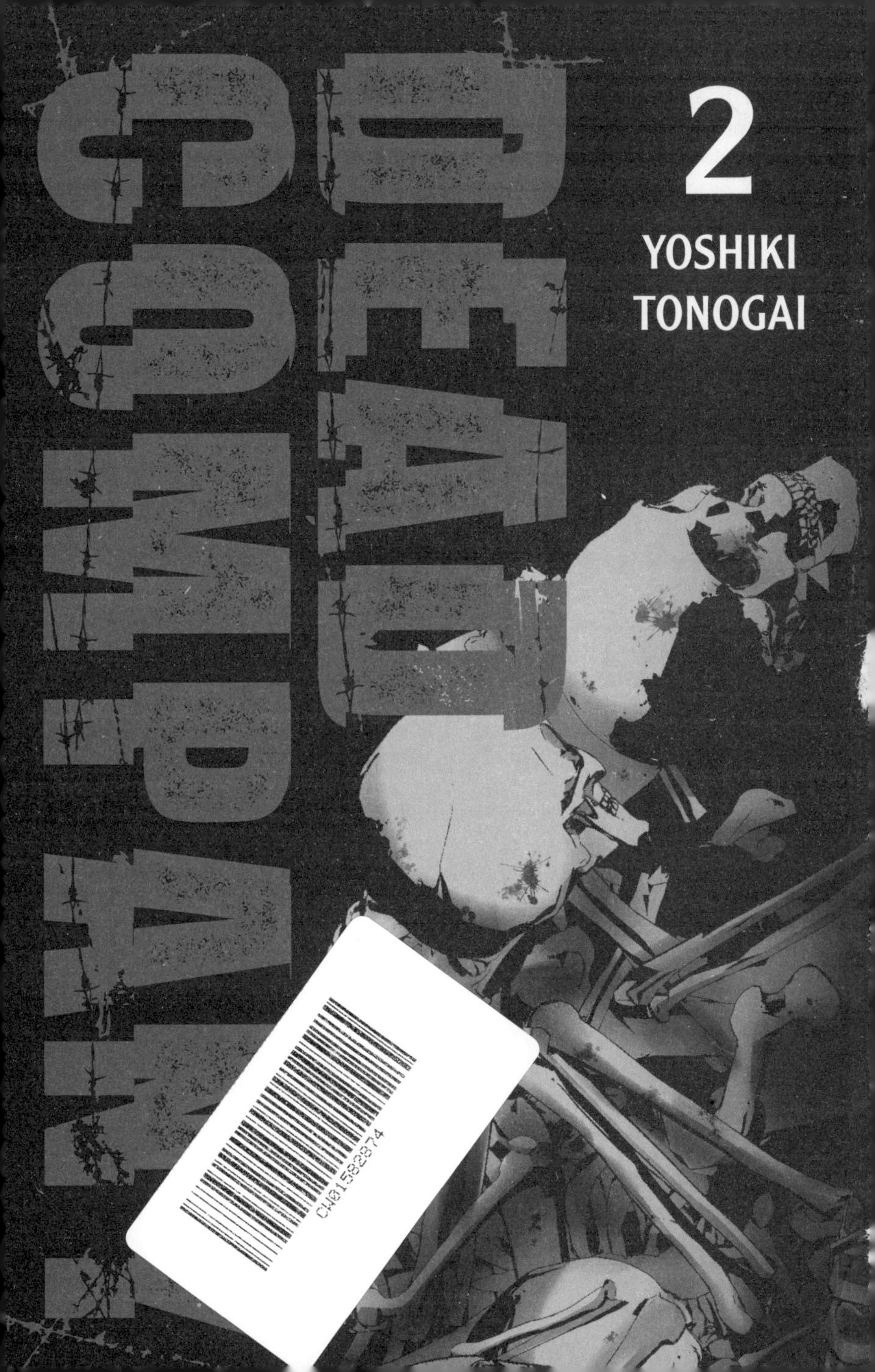
2
YOSHIKI
TONOGAI

CONTENTS

Chapter 6

* GOOD FORTUNE

HE BROUGHT ANOTHER ONE JUST LIKE IT TO WORK.
REALLY?
SMILE
I KNOW WHICH STORE SELLS THEM. LET'S GO PICK UP ANOTHER ONE FOR HIM.
WHAAAT? I'VE GOTTA GO TOO?
THINK OF IT AS THE BOTH OF US SENDING GOOD THOUGHTS TO YOUR FATHER.
WE'LL GRAB A BITE TO EAT ON OUR WAY HOME.
OH!
REALLY? LET'S GO! LET'S GO!
YOU SHOULD GET SOMETHING FOR YOUR FATHER TOO. HE'D BE THRILLED!
PITTER
PATTER
OKAY!

EXHALE
THAT SHOULD DO IT, I HOPE.
IT WOULD DEFINITELY NOT BE GOOD IF ANYBODY NOTICED BLOODSTAINS OVER HERE.
GETTING HIM INTO THE CLOSET WAS A LOT HARDER THAN I THOUGHT IT WOULD BE.
SIGH
IT'S REALLY TOUGH LUGGING SOMEONE AROUND WHEN THEY'RE JUST DEAD WEIGHT.
...
GULP
WELL, THERE'S NO GOING BACK NOW.

I'LL NEED THIS FOR LATER.
KER-CHAK
I WONDER IF THERE'S ANYTHING I CAN PUT IT IN.
!
PLUNK
IT SHOULD BE OKAY FOR NOW IF I PUT IT IN THE FRIDGE.
SALINE SOLUTION FOR CONTACT LENSES
HIGH TEMPERATURE TREATED

Chapter 6

SMILE
OKAY, PLEASE LET ME KNOW WHEN ODAGIRI WAKES UP.
ALRIGHT, WILL DO.
WHEW! I DON'T THINK SHE'S ONTO ME.
HEY, MIYAUCHI...
MAKE SURE YOU DON'T DO ANYTHING RASH, OKAY?
Relics of the

HEHEH
OTHERWISE YOU MIGHT END UP... REGRETTING IT, YOU KNOW?
Y-YEAH.
GULP
OH, BY THE WAY...
SINCE IT'S YOUR FIRST TIME HERE, I'VE SENT YOU AN E-MAIL TO SHOW YOU HOW THINGS ON THIS FLOOR WORK.
IF THERE'S ANYTHING YOU DON'T UNDERSTAND, JUST ASK ODAGIRI FOR HELP.

CLICK
SHIT! IT'S NO USE!
ALL I CAN DO FROM HERE IS MONITOR THE GAME AND FIDDLE WITH THE SETTINGS.
I CAN'T ACTUALLY STOP IT.
KYO...
WHY DID YOU AGREE TO BE A PART OF THIS?
...
CLICK
CLACK
THERE ARE SIXTEEN PLAYERS IN THIS GAME. THAT'S A LOT.

THEY CAN BEAT THIS THING IF ALL SIXTEEN OF THEM WORK TOGETHER TO ESCAPE.
ESCAPE IS THE ONLY WAY FOR ALL OF THEM TO WIN. I SHOULD BE ABLE TO DROP THEM SOME HINTS AS TIME GOES BY.
THE PROBLEM IS THAT THERE ARE FOUR KILLERS MIXED WITH THE GROUP, AND THEY HAVE THEIR OWN SPECIAL WAY OF COMMUNICATING WITH EACH OTHER.
IN ADDITION TO THE NORMAL WIN CONDITION, THE KILLERS CAN ALSO WIN IF THEY KILL EVERYBODY ELSE.
IN FACT, THEY RECEIVE A KILL BONUS FOR DOING SO.
THE DOWNSIDE TO THAT PLAN IS THAT IF TWO OR MORE OTHER PLAYERS FIGURE OUT A KILLER'S TRUE NATURE THEN THEY'LL BE FORCED TO LEAVE.
IF THINGS WERE PROCEEDING NORMALLY, THEY'D HAVE STARTED NEGOTIATING AND MANEUVERING FOR POSITION ALREADY.

BUT ONE KILLER HAS ALREADY DIED, AND THERE ARE EIGHT PLAYERS LEFT.
THE KILLERS HAVE TIPPED THEIR HAND, AND THE WHOLE GROUP HAS SPLINTERED APART.
PRETTY SOON IT WON'T MATTER WHO'S A KILLER AND WHO'S INNOCENT. IT'LL JUST TURN INTO A BLOODBATH.
GULP
AT THIS RATE, KYO WILL HAVE TO TRY TO DRAW THINGS OUT AS MUCH AS POSSIBLE.
BREATHE
THERE'S NO GOING BACK NOW.
I'VE GOT TO MAKE SURE THAT KYO IS THE LAST ONE STANDING, NO MATTER WHAT!

LOOKS LIKE IT'LL BE AN HOUR BEFORE KYO REACHES THE REST OF THE PLAYERS.
SINCE I CAN'T GET ANY INFORMATION OUT OF ODAGIRI AT THIS POINT...
I'LL JUST HAVE TO FIGURE OUT WHAT I CAN BEFORE SHE GETS THERE.
I'LL GO THROUGH THIS PLACE WITH A FINE-TOOTHED COMB.
BEEP BEEP BEEP
IT'S FROM TANAHASHI... RIGHT, THAT E-MAIL SHE MENTIONED BEFORE.
THE GUIDE FOR THIS FLOOR OR SOMETHING.

21 ··· 45
DING
1 ··· 21 ··· 45
SO THIS IS THE TWENTY-FIRST FLOOR.
CHITTER
CHATTER
THIS IS WHERE SECURITY STARTS TO GET TIGHTER.
あははっ
AH HA HA
EVERYONE HERE LOOKS SO NORMAL.
DO ALL OF THEM REALLY KNOW THE TRUTH ABOUT THIS COMPANY?
GULP

STEP
OH HEY, I HAVEN'T SEEN YOUR FACE AROUND HERE BEFORE.
SMILE
IS IT YOUR FIRST TIME HERE?
UH... YES. PRETTY MUCH ALL OF THIS IS NEW TO ME, SO I THOUGHT I'D TAKE A LOOK AT HOW THINGS WORK AROUND HERE.
IN THAT CASE, YOU SHOULD TALK TO ONE OF THE SENIOR TRAINERS.
WHO DO YOU REPORT TO?
SHOCK
GOTTA THINK OF A LIE, AND QUICK!
I'M WORKING UNDER ODAGIRI RIGHT NOW, BUT HE'S A PRETTY BUSY GUY, SO I THOUGHT I'D TRY TO FIGURE SOME STUFF OUT FOR MYSELF.
HA HA
YEAH, HE DEFINITELY COMES OFF AS A WORKAHOLIC.

IN THAT CASE, LET ME SHOW YOU AROUND. YOU DON'T KNOW MANY PEOPLE UP HERE YET, RIGHT?
IF ODAGIRI IS IN CHARGE OF YOUR TRAINING, YOU MUST BE ON THE TWENTY-FIFTH FLOOR, RIGHT? I CAN TELL YOU WHAT YOU NEED TO KNOW ABOUT THAT LEVEL.
AND IN RETURN, MAYBE YOU CAN HELP ME SLIP AWAY WITHOUT GETTING CAUGHT.
AHEM
HUH? BUT...!
THINGS ARE ABOUT TO GET HAIRY IN HERE.
CRACKLE
CRACKLE
MY NAME IS SAKURA. NICE TO MEET YOU! COME ON, LET'S GET OUT OF HERE.
HEY, WAIT A MINUTE!
PULL

ひゅー
ZIP
STOP RIGHT THERE, SAKURA!
HEY, HE'S TRYING TO GET AWAY!
WHAT?!
あはは、
HA HA HA
WHAT'S UP WITH THIS GUY?
SORRY, YOU TWO! ♪
WH–
I APPRECIATE YOU HELPING ME OUT BACK THERE.
I'LL GIVE YOU A PROPER TOUR OF THE PLACE AS A THANK YOU.

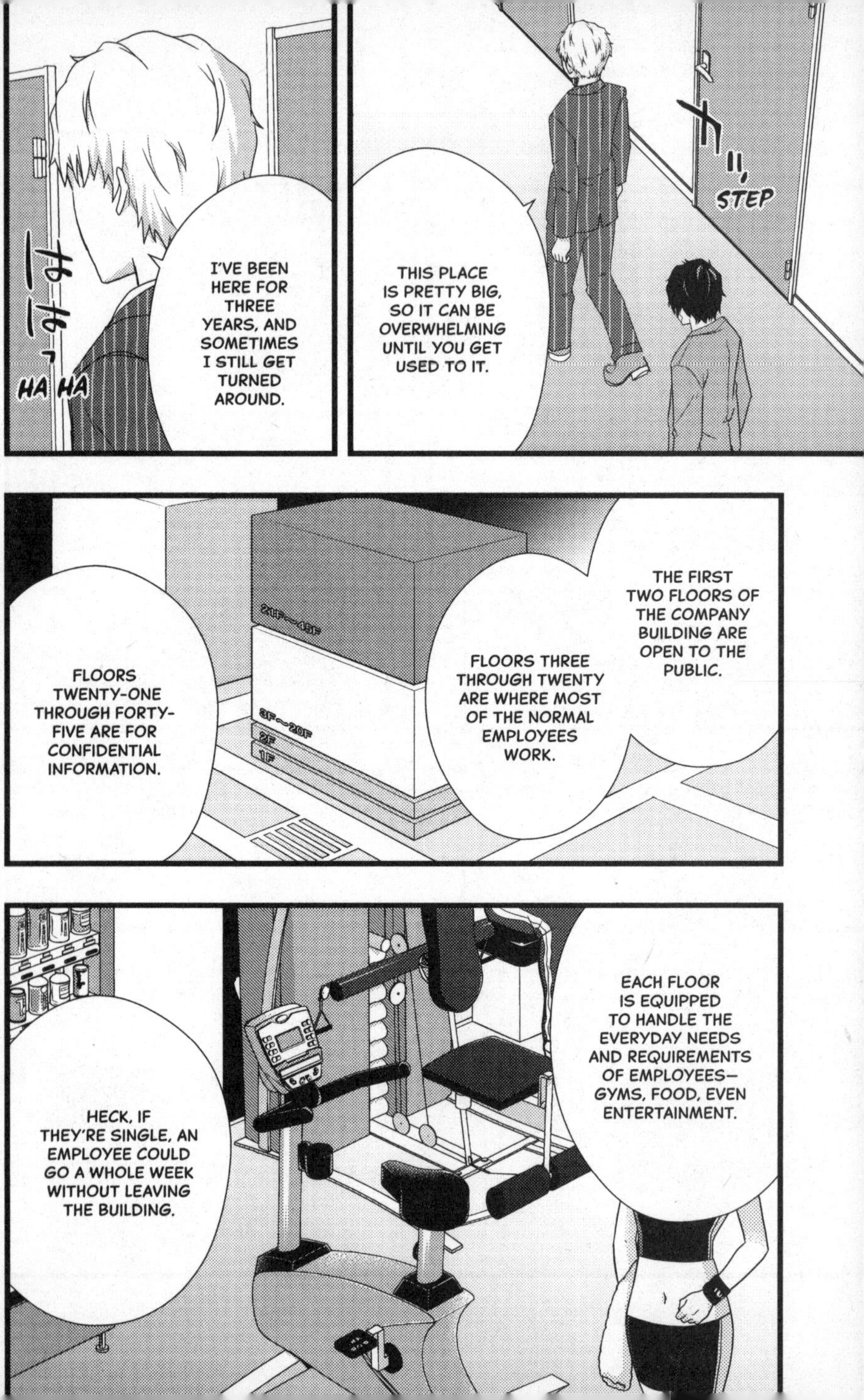
STEP
THIS PLACE IS PRETTY BIG, SO IT CAN BE OVERWHELMING UNTIL YOU GET USED TO IT.
I'VE BEEN HERE FOR THREE YEARS, AND SOMETIMES I STILL GET TURNED AROUND.
HA HA
THE FIRST TWO FLOORS OF THE COMPANY BUILDING ARE OPEN TO THE PUBLIC.
FLOORS THREE THROUGH TWENTY ARE WHERE MOST OF THE NORMAL EMPLOYEES WORK.
FLOORS TWENTY-ONE THROUGH FORTY-FIVE ARE FOR CONFIDENTIAL INFORMATION.
21F～45F
3F～20F
2F
1F
EACH FLOOR IS EQUIPPED TO HANDLE THE EVERYDAY NEEDS AND REQUIREMENTS OF EMPLOYEES—GYMS, FOOD, EVEN ENTERTAINMENT.
HECK, IF THEY'RE SINGLE, AN EMPLOYEE COULD GO A WHOLE WEEK WITHOUT LEAVING THE BUILDING.

YOU KNOW, IN CASE THEY DECIDE TO DO MORE THAN JUST ELIMINATE YOUR POSITION.
...
ガチャ
KER-CHAK
I'VE HEARD THAT THERE'S A LOUNGE, OR AN EXECUTIVE SUITE OR SOMETHING ON THE TOP FLOOR...
BUT THE LIKES OF US AREN'T ALLOWED TO GO THERE, SO BE CAREFUL NOT TO BARGE IN WHERE YOU'RE NOT PERMITTED.
UM... SAKURA?
ARE THE GAMES THAT THE COMPANY RUNS ALL HANDLED COMPLETELY IN-HOUSE?
?
YOU KNOW, LIKE CLEANING THINGS UP AFTER THE GAME IS OVER. THERE ARE CERTAIN THINGS THAT CAN ONLY BE TAKEN CARE OF ON SITE, RIGHT?

GULP
FWIP
OH, YEAH. THERE'S A SPECIALIZED CONTRACTOR THAT HANDLES THINGS LIKE THAT.
THEY'RE DIFFERENT FROM US, THOUGH. THEY'RE A BIT... EERIE I'D SAY.
YOU'RE BETTER OFF NOT KNOWING THE DETAILS.
I GUESS I DON'T HAVE ANY CHOICE BUT TO HELP HER OUT HOWEVER I CAN FROM THE TERMINAL, AND TRY TO END THE GAME WITHOUT RAISING ANY RED FLAGS.
HEY, MIYAUCHI.
SHUT
SIGH
SURE ENOUGH, SOUNDS LIKE IT'S NO USE TRYING TO GET KYO OUT WHILE THE GAME IS STILL RUNNING.

HUH?
WHAT'S ON YOUR MIND?
FLINCH
ビクッ
UM... NO... NOTHIN' REALLY?
ばっ
WHIRL
HA HA, NO NEED TO LOOK SO WORRIED.
NOBODY'S LISTENING IN ON US HERE.
CLICK
カチャ
YOU KNOW, THERE ARE QUITE A FEW PEOPLE IN THIS COMPANY WITH SENSITIVE NOSES.

IT'S DANGEROUS FOR YOU TO BE WALKING AROUND TRAILING THE SCENT OF BLOOD.

WHA–?!
SO TELL ME, MIYAUCHI...
SMIRK
WHAT ON EARTH HAVE YOU MANAGED TO SCREW UP SO BADLY?

Chapter 7

I... DON'T KNOW WHAT YOU'RE TALKING ABOUT.
WHY SO GRIM ALL OF A SUDDEN? IF THIS IS A JOKE, I DON'T GET IT.
ははっ
HA HA
AT LEAST GIVE ME A WARNING IF YOU'RE GOING TO PULL SOMETHING LIKE THAT.
GAME F...
ドキッ
BA-DUMP
ODAGIRI WAS IN CHARGE OF RUNNING THAT GAME, RIGHT?
IS IT THE *GAME* THAT YOU'RE AFTER?

I HAVE NO IDEA WHO THIS GUY IS.
BUT HE'S OBVIOUSLY FIGURED OUT WHAT I'VE DONE.
WHAT SHOULD I DO?
...
CLENCH
ギュッ
DO I HAVE TO KILL HIM NOW TOO?

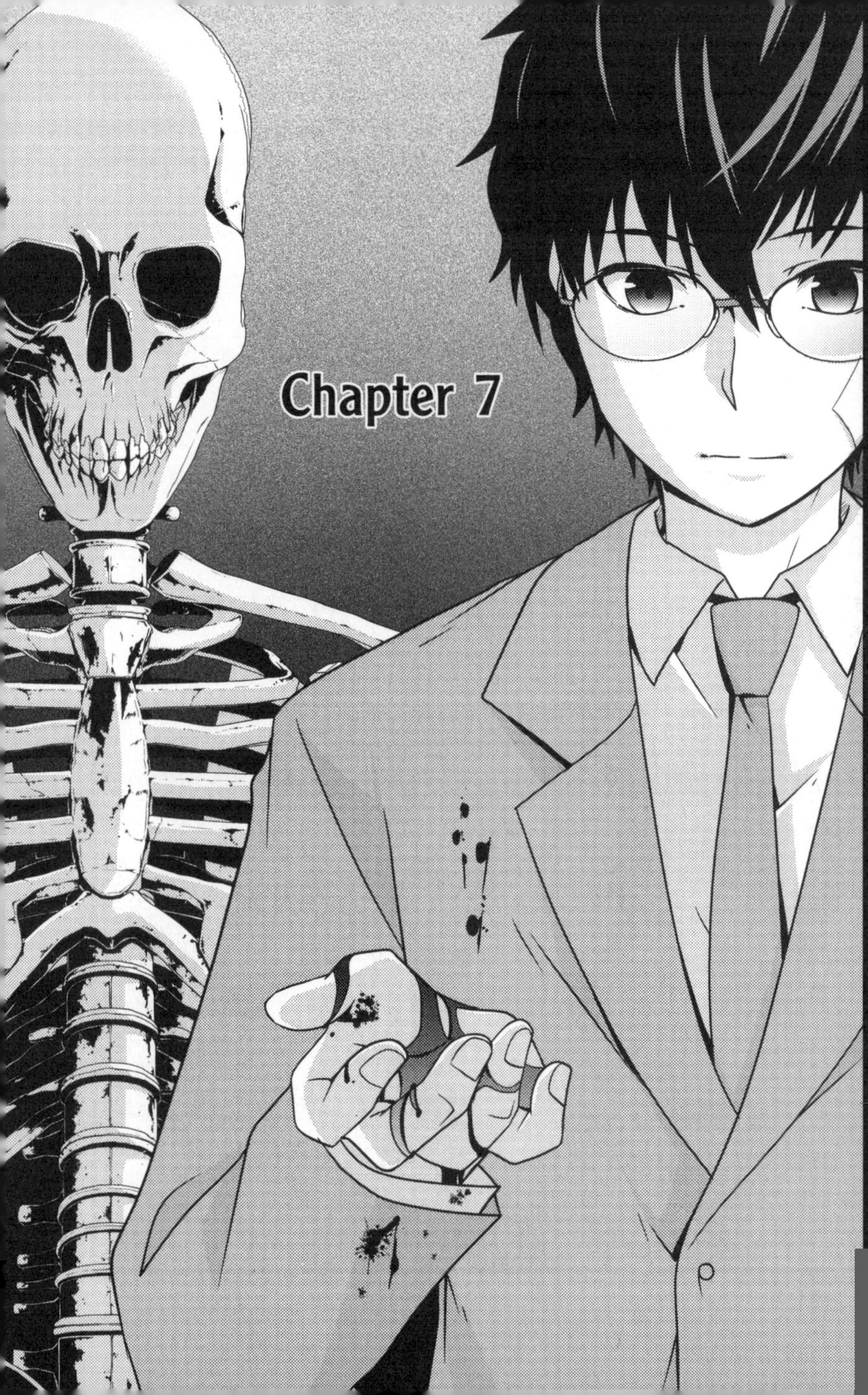
Chapter 7

I'VE ALREADY STAINED MY HANDS WITH BLOOD.
IT'S TOO LATE TO GET COLD FEET.
I HOPE YOU'RE NOT THINKING OF DOING ANYTHING... HASTY.
HMPH

FWIP
I CAN CALL DOWN A SECURITY TEAM WITH THE TOUCH OF A BUTTON.
I WONDER WHAT THEY'D DO TO SOMEONE WHO TRIED MOVING AGAINST THE COMPANY?
YOU KNOW THE SORT OF THING OUR COMPANY DOES, RIGHT?
THEY'D PROBABLY MAKE YOU A TEST SUBJECT FOR THE DRUGS THEY USE IN THE DEATH GAMES.
DID YOU KNOW THERE ARE CERTAIN DRUGS THAT CAN KEEP YOU CAUGHT BETWEEN LIFE AND DEATH? WHO KNOWS HOW LONG THEY COULD DRAW OUT YOUR SUFFERING?
DON'T GO THINKING THEY'D LET YOU HAVE AN EASY DEATH.
GULP

THEY'D TELL YOUR FAMILY THAT YOU'D GONE MISSING...
AND THE WORLD WOULD FORGET YOU EVEN EXISTED.
YOU DON'T WANT THAT TO HAPPEN, DO YOU?
...
MOM...
STILL, I'VE GOTTA TRY.
IF I CAN GET TO THAT FIRE EXTINGUISHER BEFORE HE CAN ACT, MAYBE I CAN KNOCK HIM DOWN.
GLANCE
チラ
FIRE EXTINGUISHER

TELL YOU WHAT, IF YOU'RE STRAIGHT WITH ME ABOUT WHAT HAPPENED, I'LL GIVE YOU A CHANCE.
A CHANCE?
TELL ME AN INTERESTING ENOUGH STORY, AND I'LL OVERLOOK WHAT YOU'VE DONE.
ACTUALLY, I'LL DO BETTER THAN THAT. I'LL EVEN HELP YOU OUT.
WHAT'S WITH THIS GUY?

HA HA HA HA HA!
SORRY FOR LAUGHING.
はぁ PANT
はぁ PANT
I DIDN'T EXPECT SUCH A STRAIGHT-FORWARD REASON OUT OF YOU.
SO, YOU DID IT TO HELP SOMEONE OUT.
STILL, GOING SO FAR AS TO KILL YOUR SUPERVISOR IS A BIT EXTREME, DON'T YOU THINK?
...

WELL, I TOLD YOU EVERYTHING, JUST LIKE YOU ASKED.
WAVE
ば
WERE YOU JUST LYING TO ME WHEN YOU SAID YOU'D GIVE ME A BREAK?
TRUE, TRUE... WELL, IN YOUR CASE I GUESS IT'S OKAY.
AS IT STANDS, IT'S ONLY A MATTER OF TIME UNTIL WORD GETS OUT THAT YOU KILLED ODAGIRI.
...
REACH
SO I'LL DO THIS TO HELP YOU OUT.
BEEP

WHAT WAS THAT?
WELL, I JUST SO HAPPEN TO BE PART OF THE SECURITY DIVISION.
I JUST GAVE YOUR RETINAL PROFILE ACCESS TO ODAGIRI'S ROOM.
!
YOU SHOULDN'T UNDERESTIMATE OUR SECURITY SYSTEM HERE.
THE RETINAL RECOGNITION SYSTEM IS STATE-OF-THE-ART. IT WILL THROW UP A RED FLAG IF IT DETECTS EVEN THE SMALLEST ABNORMALITY.
IN THIS CASE, I RECEIVED AN ALERT THAT THERE WAS A READING OUTSIDE THE MARGIN OF ERROR.
パチッ
WINK

YOU SEE, ONE TIME THERE WAS A DEATH GAME WHERE RETINAL SCANS CAME INTO PLAY.
THERE WAS A PLAYER WHO TOOK OUT SOMEONE'S EYEBALL AND TRIED TO USE IT, JUST LIKE YOU DID.
IT WAS ACTUALLY THANKS TO THE DATA THAT WE GATHERED BACK THEN THAT THE SECURITY SYSTEM PICKED UP ON YOUR TRICK THIS TIME.
HUH? THEN WHAT WAS ALL THAT "I CAN SMELL THE BLOOD ON YOU" STUFF ABOUT?
クスッ
SNICKER
THAT WAS JUST A BLUFF.
WHAT?!
I DIDN'T THINK YOU'D COME CLEAN WITH ME UNLESS I SAID SOMETHING LIKE THAT.
ははっ
HA HA

SORRY FOR THREATENING YOU BACK THERE.
...
SAKURA...
WHY DIDN'T YOU REPORT ME TO THE COMPANY?
I MEAN, YOU'RE EVEN *HELPING* ME.
GULP
WHAT THE HECK ARE YOU THINKING?

ははっ
HA HA
COME ON NOW, DON'T LOOK SO SERIOUS.
LET YOUR GUARD DOWN A LITTLE BIT.
AFTER ALL, THERE'S MORE I CAN DO TO HELP YOU OUT HERE.
HELP ME *HOW?*
YOUR WAY OF DOING THINGS IS A BIT ROUGH AROUND THE EDGES, YOU KNOW?
IF YOU KEEP THIS UP, IT'S ONLY A MATTER OF TIME BEFORE SOMEONE OTHER THAN ME CATCHES ON.
パチッ
SNAP
THAT'S WHY I'LL BE SUPPORTING YOU FROM BEHIND THE SCENES.
THERE ARE A LOT OF NASTY CHARACTERS IN OUR COMPANY, YOU KNOW.

FWIP
OF COURSE, I'LL NEED YOU TO DO SOMETHING IN RETURN.
YOU SEE, THERE'S A CERTAIN REQUEST I HAVE FOR YOU.
A REQUEST?
DON'T WORRY, IT'S NOTHING THAT WILL GET IN THE WAY OF YOUR OWN GOALS.
SMILE
THERE'S A SOMETHING I'D LIKE THE TWO OF US TO DO TOGETHER.
OH YEAH?

LET'S TAKE THIS COMPANY DOWN.
...

BEEEP
KER-CHAK
!
CREEAAAAK
I GUESS THAT'S SUPPOSED TO MEAN "GET IN THERE."
GULP
ONCE I GO THROUGH THAT DOOR, I'LL BE ANOTHER PLAYER IN THE DEATH GAME.

YOU WANT ME TO BE IN A... DEATH GAME?
WE FEEL THAT YOUR ASSISTANCE WOULD BE INDISPENSIBLE.
MISS MIWA?
...
WHY WOULD YOU CHOOSE ME?
THE COMPANY IS UNDERSTAFFED AT THE MOMENT, SO I'M AFRAID ALL OF OUR PERSONNEL ARE EXTREMELY BUSY.
ははっ
HA HA
AND I JUST HAPPENED TO REMEMBER YOU.
Menu
Menu

IF YOU'RE WILLING TO ACCEPT OUR PROPROSAL...
I'M PREPARED TO GIVE YOU THE INFORMATION THAT YOU HAD PREVIOUSLY REQUESTED.
TWITCH
SO, WHAT DO YOU WANT ME TO DO?
HA HA, NOW THAT'S THE SPIRIT!
OUR COMPANY'S OBJECTIVE IS TO CREATE DEATH GAMES THAT MAXIMIZE THE CRUELTY AND ENTERTAINMENT FACTORS FOR PLAYERS.
CLATTER
AT THE MOMENT, THERE'S ONE THING IN PARTICULAR WE WOULD LIKE YOU TO DO.

...
BREATHE
SO, MY JOB IS TO KEEP THE TWO SIDES HERE EVENLY BALANCED SO THAT THE GAME WILL LAST AS LONG AS POSSIBLE.
I'LL REALLY BE PLAYING WITH FIRE HERE.
GULP
THEN THERE'S ONE MORE THING...
KER-CHAK

I GUESS YER THE NEW PLAYER THEY'RE THROWIN' IN HERE.
STARE

HEY, SHE'S A CUTIE, AIN'T SHE?
GEEZ, DO YOU HAVE TO BE SO SHALLOW ALL THE TIME?
SHUDDER
?!
AAAAAHHH!
YER A LOUD ONE. COOL YER JETS ALREADY.
COME ON, THAT'S HOW ANYONE *NORMAL* WOULD REACT.

WE'RE BETTER OFF WITH SOMEONE LIKE THAT THAN SOME IDIOT WHO THINKS THEY CAN SOLVE EVERYTHING WITH FORCE...
LIKE THIS GUY RIGHT HERE.
NUDGE
I DON'T KNOW WHO GOT HIM, BUT I'M GRATEFUL TO THEM.
HEY, YER PRETTY ROUGH YERSELF.
WHAT? THERE'S ALREADY BEEN ANOTHER VICTIM?
WHAT SHOULD I DO? I HAVE TO DO SOMETHING.
IF THE DEATH GAME ENDS TOO QUICKLY, THAT MEANS I'VE FAILED.
CLENCH

ピトッ
TAP
...
THAT GIRL...!
GULP
ゴクッ
THAT'S RIGHT. SHE'S THE ONE WHO KILLED THIS GUY.

SHE'S ALREADY KILLED THREE OTHER PEOPLE.
YOU'LL HAVE TO GET CLOSE TO HER FIRST AND OBSERVE HER BEHAVIOR.
GULP
WITH HIS HELP, MAYBE I CAN DO IT.
DON'T WORRY, I'M HERE TO SUPPORT YOU.

I'M YOUR OPERATOR. BELIEVE IN ME, AND WE'LL GET THROUGH THIS!
OKAY.
WE CAN DO THIS.

SNICKER
クスッ
THIS WILL DO NICELY.
SO, HE'S RISKING HIS NECK TO SAVE THE SISTER OF THE WOMAN HE LOVED.
スッ
FWIP
I'M A BIT SUPRISED THAT THINGS ARE ACTUALLY GOING AS PLANNED.
ガチャ
KER-CHAK
I WAS SURPRISED WHEN I FIRST HEARD ABOUT YOU.
ASKING THAT GIRL FROM HR TO ASSIGN ME TO ODAGIRI'S UNIT HAS WORKED OUT WELL.
BRINGING DOWN THIS COMPANY WILL BE A LOT EASIER WITH MIYAUCHI'S HELP.

NEW OPTIONS ARE OPEN TO ME NOW THAT I HAVE AT LEAST ONE OTHER PERSON AT MY DISPOSAL.
HEHEH
A PROMISE IS A PROMISE, SO I'LL HELP MAKE SURE THE GIRL GETS OUT OF THE GAME ALIVE.
STEP
HOWEVER...
WHETHER THE TWO OF THEM CAN SURVIVE AFTER THAT IS NONE OF MY CONCERN.

STEP
HEY.
GLANCE
OH, HELLO SAKURA.
?
THAT'S THE ELEVATOR FOR THE EXECUTIVE LEVEL, RIGHT?
IS HE ALLOWED TO USE THAT?
YOU MEAN YOU DON'T KNOW?
SAKURA IS SPECIAL, SO IT'S OKAY.
WHAT DO YOU MEAN?

はぁ
SIGH
I WAS JUST STARTING TO ENJOY WATCHING MIYAUCHI AT WORK. JUST MY LUCK.
WHY DID THAT PAIN-IN-THE-NECK HAVE TO CALL FOR ME NOW?
DING
HEY, YOU MADE IT UP HERE QUICKLY.
NICE HUSTLE.
GOOD MORNING, SUZUKI.

SO, HOW'S WORK GOING?
I'VE BEEN LEARNING BIT BY BIT FROM MY MORE EXPERIENCED COLLEAGUES.
HA HA
HUMBLE TO A FAULT, AS USUAL. YOU SHOULD STOP BEING SO MODEST ALL THE TIME.
NO ONE WOULD HOLD IT AGAINST YOU, SEEING AS HOW YOU'LL BE IN CHARGE ONE DAY.
HMPH
WHAT AN ASS-KISSER.
KNOCK
KNOCK
COME IN.
KER-CHAK
EXCUSE ME, SIR. I'VE BROUGHT SAKURA, LIKE YOU ASKED.

SHUT
SORRY TO HAVE KEPT YOU WAITING, SIR.
YOU MAY GO, SUZUKI.
STRAIGHTEN
AS YOU WISH, SIR.
I MEAN, FATHER.
CREAK

Chapter 8

WHEN WE WOKE UP, WE WERE ALL TRAPPED IN HERE.
はぁ
SIGH
AND WHY THE HELL DO WE HAVE TO DO WHAT THAT CREEP SAYS?

WHO?
THERE WAS SOME GUY ON THE MONITOR WHEN WE CAME TO. HE WAS THERE TO EXPLAIN THE RULES OF THE GAME.
HE HAD SOME SORT OF CREEPY RABBIT MASK ON.
A RABBIT...!
GULP
DOES THAT MEAN IT WAS THE SAME GUY WHO WAS CALLING THE SHOTS IN MY GAME?
YOU SAID YOUR NAME WAS KAGESAKI, RIGHT?
Y-YEAH.

HOW ABOUT WORKING TOGETHER WITH US, SO WE CAN GET THROUGH THIS THING?
HUH?
HMPH
YEAH, THAT'D BE GOOD. THOSE OTHER GUYS ARE A BUNCH OF USELESS LUMPS.
YOU DIDN'T THINK THEY WERE KINDA LIKE US?
GRR
SAY WHAT?
DON'T GO COMPARING ME TO THOSE WORTHLESS SHITS!
GULP
WH-WHAT SHOULD I DO?
I WOULDN'T PUT TOO MUCH TRUST IN THOSE THREE IF I WERE YOU.

THAT'S SHINJI KINJO. HE'S ON THE RUN FROM THE POLICE AFTER BEING CHARGED WITH ROBBERY.
HE HAS A SHORT TEMPER, AND HIS CRIMINAL RECORD SHOWS HE ISN'T SHY ABOUT RESORTING TO VIOLENCE.
THEN THERE'S RYO MINAGAWA. SHE HEADS UP A SCAMMING NETWORK WITH THE YAKUZA.
FINALLY, THAT'S AINA YUKIMURA. SHE'S THE ONE WHO'S RESPONSIBLE FOR THE DEAD GUY AT YOUR FEET.
BEFORE SHE GOT HERE, SHE STALKED THREE OTHER PEOPLE AND DROVE THEM TO SUICIDE.
BE ESPECIALLY CAREFUL AROUND HER.
GULP

SO, FIRST—
AH, UM... I'M GRATEFUL FOR THE OFFER...
BUT DO YOU THINK I COULD MEET THE OTHERS FIRST BEFORE MAKING A DECISION?
SURE, IF YOU WANT TO.
はあ SIGH
WE'VE GOTTA LET THEM KNOW THAT THIS GUY'S DEAD ANYWAY.
THAT OKAY WITH YOU, YUKIMURA?
コクッ NOD
PHEW ホッ

GO ALONG WITH THE THREE OF THEM.
IF POSSIBLE, SEE IF YOU CAN FISH AROUND FOR SOME DETAILS ABOUT WHAT'S HAPPENED SO FAR IN THIS DEATH GAME.
GOTCHA.
WHISPER
I'M SORRY TO BE RELYING SO MUCH ON SOMEONE I'M JUST TALKING TO FOR THE FIRST TIME.
TWITCH
DON'T WORRY ABOUT IT.
IT'S MY JOB TO HELP YOU OUT.
YEAH, WELL THANKS ANYWAY.

THERE'S SOMEBODY THAT I WANT TO MEET ONCE I'VE FINISHED THIS JOB.
I'M NOT GOING TO LET MYSELF DIE IN HERE.
...
DOES SHE MEAN...?
GRIP
ギュッ
NO, BETTER NOT THINK ABOUT THAT NOW.
FOR NOW I JUST NEED TO FOCUS ON KEEPING KYO ALIVE AND GETTING HER OUT OF THIS DEATH GAME.

STEP
I WONDER WHAT THIS BUILDING IS.
IT'S GOTTA BE SOME PLACE UNDERGROUND. THERE AREN'T ANY WINDOWS.
IT'S BEEN THREE DAYS SINCE WE GOT HERE. I COULD REALLY USE SOME FRESH AIR.
HRMPH
THREE DAYS?
IT'S BEEN THAT LONG? WHAT ARE YOU DOING FOR FOOD AND STUFF?
WELL, WE MANAGE.
JUST MANAGING TO SURVIVE IS ALSO PART OF THE DEATH GAME.
SIGH

TAKE A LOOK. THE FACILITY IS DIVIDED INTO A FEW DIFFERENT AREAS.
EACH AREA HAS ITS OWN LOCK, SO AT FIRST WE COULDN'T MOVE BETWEEN THEM.
WE DECIDED TO SPLIT UP SO WE COULD FIND A WAY TO UNLOCK THE DOORS.
THERE ARE ALSO GENERATOR ROOMS LIKE THIS.
WHENEVER WE GET ONE OF 'EM GOING AGAIN, WE CAN TURN THE WATER BACK ON AND GET ACCESS TO ANY FOOD THAT'S IN THE AREA.
OH, PERFECT TIMING. TAKE A LOOK AT THIS.
SLOW

WHAT? DON'T LOOK SO SKEPTICAL.
IT'S JUST A BIT... UNEXPECTED TO FIND ALL OF YOU COOPERATING WITH ONE ANOTHER.
THIS PLACE IS PRETTY BIG. WE ALL WANT TO GET OUT OF HERE, AND WE ALL NEED TO EAT TOO. WE'VE GOTTA HELP EACH OTHER OUT.
チャ
CLICK
PLUS...
GASP
HE'S GOT A PISTOL?!

THERE'S A CHANCE OF FINDING MORE WEAPONS LIKE THIS WHEN WE GET TO A NEW FLOOR. THAT'S WHY EVERYONE'S SO EAGER TO GET MOVING.
LISTEN, KINJO. IF YOU'VE GOT THE GUN, YOU SHOULD BE USING IT MORE.
QUIT TALKIN' CRAZY.
THEY WEREN'T TOO GENEROUS WITH THE AMMO. I'VE ONLY GOT THREE SHOTS LEFT.
FWIP
THIS IS ONLY FOR THREATENIN' FOLKS AND SAVING MY OWN HIDE.
I KNOW SOME PEOPLE GOT THEIR HANDS ON STUN GUNS AND KNIVES...
BUT I'M SURE THERE ARE FOLKS THAT ARE HIDING WEAPONS WITHOUT TELLING ANYBODY.
THAT DEAD GUY BACK THERE? TSUTSUI? WHOEVER KILLED HIM USED POISON.
OH!

DID YOU SAY... POISON?
チラ
GLANCE
THERE WERE OTHERS WHO DIED OF POISON EARLIER.
WHIRL
クル
SINCE THEN, WE'VE BEEN KEEPING AN EYE ON WHO'S HOLDING THE FOOD AND WHO IT GETS PASSED TO.
AND TSUTSUI *STILL* GOT HIMSELF POISONED.
HE MUST'VE STOLEN SOME FOOD THAT WE FOUND IN AN EARLIER BLOCK.
KYO, RIGHT? YOU SHOULD MAKE SURE TO KEEP AN EYE ON YOUR OWN FOOD.
OKAY...

POISONING...
THAT MUST'VE BEEN YUKIMURA'S DOING, RIGHT?
YEAH. THAT'S WHAT THE LOG HERE SHOWS.
THE PLAYERS WHO ARE SEASONED KILLERS HAVE BEEN TOLD FROM THE START WHERE DIFFERENT WEAPONS ARE SQUIRRELED AWAY.
SHE MUST'VE FOUND POISON IN ONE OF THOSE CACHES.
STEP
FOR NOW, JUST AVOID ANY FOOD THAT YUKIMURA HAS TOUCHED.
GOT IT.
YOU'D BETTER KEEP AN EYE ON THAT KINJO GUY TOO.
?

HE WAS LYING WHEN HE SAID HE ONLY HAD THREE SHOTS LEFT IN HIS PISTOL.
HE REALLY HAS FOUR.
I CAN CHECK ON ALL SORTS OF INFORMATION ABOUT THE GAME FROM MY SYSTEM HERE.
NOD
BE CAREFUL YOU DON'T REVEAL ANY INFORMATION THAT YOU SHOULDN'T KNOW.
CREEEEAAAAK

LOOKS LIKE THE REST OF 'EM AREN'T HERE YET.
I NEED TO USE THE BATHROOM.
STEP
AW MAN, I WANTED TO TAKE A LEAK FIRST.
FWUMP
IT'S NOT MUCH, BUT YOU SHOULD SIT DOWN AND RELAX WHILE YOU CAN.
OH, TH-THANK YOU.
KER-CHAK

RUSH
LOOKS LIKE THIS WAS THE RIGHT WAY.
WE WERE ABLE TO GET TO A NEW BLOCK, SO WE SHOULD BE ABLE TO—
WHO THE HECK ARE YOU?
UH... UM... I'M...!
STEP
SHE MUST BE THE NEW PLAYER THAT THE ANNOUNCEMENT WAS TALKING ABOUT.
THEY'RE ADDING HER IN THE MIDDLE OF THE GAME, SO SHE MUST NOT BE ONE OF THE KILLERS. THAT'S A RELIEF!

WHY?
WHAT ARE YOU DOING HERE...
?
MEGUMI?

THAT GIRL...
Chapter 9
WASN'T SHE ONE OF KYO'S FRIENDS FROM THE OTHER NIGHT?
WHAT ARE YOU DOING HERE?
STRIDE
BLOCK
?

WHAT DO YOU THINK YOU'RE DOING?
SHE'S WITH US...
SO DON'T JUST MARCH OVER HERE AND START TALKING AT HER.
OF COURSE, IF YOU JOINED UP WITH US IT WOULDN'T BE AN ISSUE.
SMIRK
WH–?
ATTENTION PLAYERS: I'D LIKE TO INFORM YOU ALL ABOUT WHAT HAS TRANSPIRED TODAY.

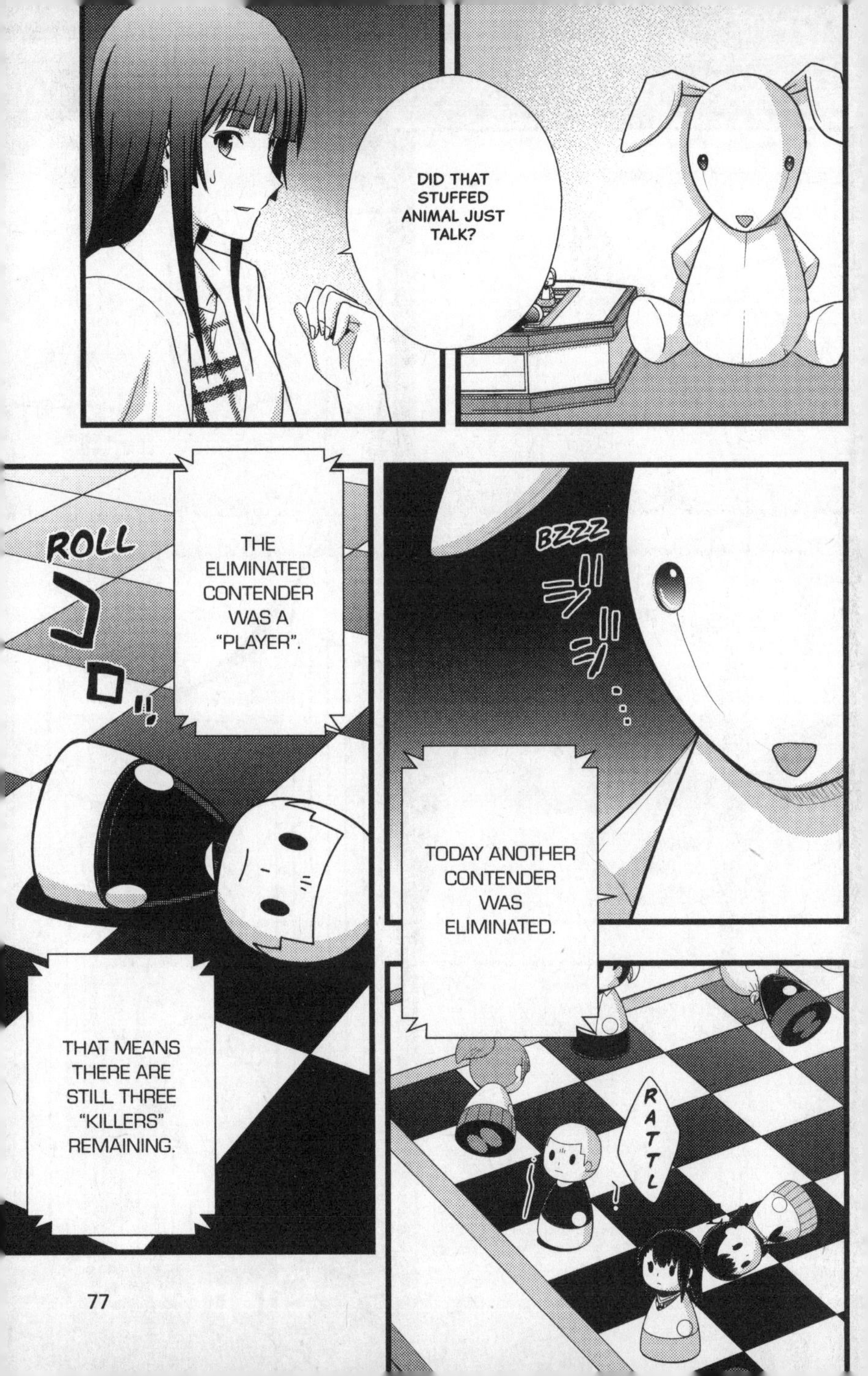
DID THAT STUFFED ANIMAL JUST TALK?
BZZZ
TODAY ANOTHER CONTENDER WAS ELIMINATED.
ROLL
THE ELIMINATED CONTENDER WAS A "PLAYER".
RATTL
THAT MEANS THERE ARE STILL THREE "KILLERS" REMAINING.

Chapter 9

WHINE
THERE'S ALSO ONE MORE THING FOR TODAY. AS PREVIOUSLY ANNOUNCED, A NEW PLAYER HAS BEEN ADDED.
カチ CLICK
!
IT LOOKS LIKE THERE'S ANOTHER PIECE ON THE BOARD, NOW THAT YOU'VE JOINED, UH...?
カチャ CLICK
IS THAT SUPPOSED TO BE ME?
THEY LOOK JUST LIKE US, DON'T THEY? THEY PUT WAY TOO MUCH EFFORT INTO THESE THINGS. THEY'RE SUPPOSED TO REPRESENT US IN THE GAME, SEE?
KYO. MY NAME IS KYO KAGESAKI.

THE FIRST VICTIM WAS BEATEN TO DEATH. THE SECOND AND THIRD VICTIMS WERE POISONED.
THE FOURTH VICTIM WAS STRANGLED. THE FIFTH KILLED THEMSELVES.
THE SIXTH ONE WAS ELECTROCUTED, WHILE THE SEVENTH ONE WAS CRUSHED BY A COLLAPSING WALL.
THE EIGHTH DIED OF UNKNOWN CAUSES, AND THE NINTH...

AND THE NINTH ONE... THIS IS TSUTSUI'S FIGURINE, RIGHT?
WOAH!
KINJO, WHY'D THE OLD DUDE DIE?
IT WAS POISON. IT MUST'VE BEEN FROM SOME FOOD THAT HE'D STOLEN.
REALLY? WHAT AN IDIOT.
WE ALL KNEW THAT WAS A RISK. THAT'S WHY WE CAME UP WITH THE WHOLE ROUTINE OF PREPARING FOOD AS A GROUP AND DOLING IT OUT AT RANDOM.
WE'VE ALL GOT TO WORK TOGETHER TO STAND AGAINST THE KILLERS.
WHAT'S WITH THIS GUY?
SOMEBODY JUST DIED! WHY IS HE SO CHEERFUL?

WELL, AT LEAST THIS MAKES IT EASY FOR US TO UNDERSTAND WHAT'S GOING ON.
IF SOMEONE'S PIECE FALLS OVER, WE KNOW THEY'RE DEAD!
AND THIS STUFFED ANIMAL GIVES US A REPORT EVERY DAY ON HOW THE GAME IS PROGRESSING.
THE LAST ANNOUNCEMENT OF THE DAY TELLS US IF ANY OF THE PEOPLE WHO DIED THAT DAY WERE KILLERS.
ALSO—
CRACKLE
SINCE YOU HAVE BEEN FOLLOWING THE RULES, I WILL NOW OPEN A NEW DOOR.

I WILL ALSO CONFIRM ONCE AGAIN THAT KYO KAGESAKI IS NOT ONE OF THE "KILLERS."
...
THE SURVIVING "PLAYERS" SHOULD WORK WITH HER TO ESCAPE THE FACILITY.
THE THREE REMAINING "KILLERS" SHOULD MAKE AN EFFORT TO COORDINATE THEIR ACTIONS.
WELL THEN...
I'LL BE EXPECTING YOU ALL TO MAKE THIS AN ENTERTAINING DEATH GAME.

SILENCE
SEE, WHAT'D I TELL YA?
ALL THAT DOLL DOES IS SPOUT OUT BULLSHIT.
HMPH
?
THAT GUY'S STILL ANGRY ABOUT WHAT IT SAID AT THE START OF THE GAME.
"ONLY THE WICKED HAVE BEEN INVITED TO THIS DEATH GAME."
HEH

LISTEN, I DON'T MIND BEING TREATED LIKE A BAD GUY.
I KNOW I'M NO ANGEL, BUT HOW IS THAT A REASON FOR PUTTING US ALL THROUGH THIS?
COULD MEGUMI REALLY BE A "WICKED" PERSON?
I MEAN, I'VE HEARD SOME PRETTY WILD RUMORS ABOUT HER, BUT...
SHOCK
?!
SHE COULDN'T BE A KILLER, COULD SHE?

GRAB
DON'T WORRY, SHE'S NOT ONE OF THE KILLERS.
PHEW
OKAY, WELL IF WE WORK WITH MEGUMI—
HUH? WHAT IS IT, MINAGAWA?
LOOK, IT SEEMS LIKE YOU KNOW THAT GIRL, BUT STOP RIGHT THERE.
WE DON'T REALLY TRUST EACH OTHER EVEN WITHIN OUR *OWN* GROUP.
WE CAN'T JUST GO AHEAD AND BRING OVER SOMEONE FROM *THEIR* GROUP.
BESIDES, THE LESS WE HAVE TO DO WITH *THOSE* TWO THE BETTER.

THAT GUY WITH THE CRAZY EYES IS TACHIBANA.
HE KILLED A GUY RIGHT IN FRONT OF EVERYBODY.
BACK WHEN THE DEATH GAME FIRST STARTED, THERE WAS THIS GUY WITH GLASSES WHO TRIED TO TAKE CHARGE OF THINGS.
TACHIBANA DIDN'T TAKE KINDLY TO THAT...
AND BEAT THE GUY TO DEATH RIGHT THEN AND THERE BEFORE THE RULES HAD EVEN BEEN EXPLAINED.

TACHIBANA USED TO BE A PROFESSIONAL BOXER.
HE'D BREAK THE RULES DURING MATCHES BY NOT LETTING HIS OPPONENT GET BACK UP, AND OTHER SIMILAR STUNTS.
HE WAS REPEATEDLY INVOLVED IN EXCESSIVELY VIOLENT INCIDENTS UNTIL THEY EVENTUALLY STRIPPED HIM OF HIS LICENSE.
JUST LIKE MINAGAWA SAID, IT'S BEST NOT TO TRY TO STAND UP TO HIM RIGHT NOW.
GULP
EVEN SO, TACHIBANA ISN'T ONE OF THE KILLERS. HE'S JUST AN EXCEPTIONALLY VIOLENT PLAYER.
YOSHINO, THE GUY NEXT TO HIM, IS THE ONE TO LOOK OUT FOR.
HE'S ONE OF THE KILLERS.

YOSHINO HAS THE SAME SORT OF VIOLENT TENDENCIES AS TACHIBANA, BUT HE'S NOT PARTICULARLY STRONG.
CLICK
CLICK
HE'S GOT A NASTY HABIT OF FINDING PEOPLE THAT ARE WEAKER THAN HIM AND TORMENTING THEM MERCILESSLY.
ACCORDING TO THE LOGS, HE'S THE ONE WHO GAVE MEGUMI THAT CUT ON HER FACE.
OH NO...
I KNOW IT'S HARD TO SEE YOUR FRIEND GET HURT, BUT THAT'S NOTHING TO A GUY LIKE YOSHINO.
WE STILL HAVE TO GET A SENSE OF WHAT'S GOING ON, SO YOU'LL JUST HAVE TO SIT ON THOSE FEELINGS FOR NOW.
GOT IT.
GRIP
HUH?

WHAT'S UP?
WHAT?! OH... NOTHING.
INCLUDING ME, THERE SHOULD BE EIGHT PEOPLE LEFT. WE'RE MISSING SOMEONE.
?
YOU'RE RIGHT... SOMEBODY'S MISSING.
DOES THAT MEAN THAT THE THIRD KILLER IS ACTING ON THEIR OWN?
YOU'RE BETTER OFF LEAVING THAT GUY ALONE.
HE ALWAYS DOES HIS OWN THING. OR AT LEAST HE'S BEEN GOING IT ALONE SO FAR.

THERE ARE TIMES IN THIS DEATH GAME THAT YOU HAVE TO COOPERATE WITH OTHER PEOPLE TO GET ANYWHERE.
YOU KNOW, LIKE PRESSING TWO DIFFERENT SWITCHES AT THE SAME TIME AND OTHER SIMILAR PUZZLES.
TAP
SO SOMETIMES WE HAVE TO TRY WORKING WITH HIM ANYWAY, EVEN THOUGH HE'S PRETTY UNRELIABLE.
BUT FOR REAL, THAT DUDE IS SERIOUSLY WEIRD. WATCH YOURSELF AROUND HIM, KAGESAKI.
ANYWAY, HOW ABOUT JOINING UP WITH US?
TACHIBANA IS SUPER STRONG, SO HE'S COMFORTING TO HAVE AROUND.

SEEMS LIKE YOU'RE FRIENDS WITH MEGUMI TOO.
YOU'D DEFINITELY HAVE MORE FUN BEING WITH US.
GRIN
N-NO... THANKS, THOUGH.
REALLY? THAT'S TOO BAD. JUST LET US KNOW IF YOU CHANGE YOUR MIND.
THAT GOES FOR YOU TOO, MINAGAWA.
はぁ
SIGH
WHO'D WANT TO WORK WITH YOU?
THAT'S HARSH, MAN.
SO, THIS GUY, YUKIMURA, AND THE GUY WHO'S NOT HERE ARE THE THREE KILLERS.

ALRIGHT, IT LOOKS LIKE THE THREE REMAINING KILLERS EACH HAVE SOME KIND OF MINIATURE COMMUNICATION DEVICE.
THAT'S PROBABLY HOW THEY'RE ABLE TO COORDINATE THEIR MOVES.
"PROBABLY"?
APPARENTLY THEY WERE DISTRIBUTED RANDOMLY, SO EVEN AN ADMINISTRATOR WOULDN'T KNOW EXACTLY WHO HAS WHAT.
THE DEVICES CAN LOOK LIKE ANYTHING, LIKE A WATCH OR A CARD.
GLANCE
UNDERSTOOD. I'LL BE CAREFUL WHEN I'M OBSERVING THEM.
SO, THERE'S ONE MORE KILLER...
CLICK

BE-BEEP
HOW DOES THAT SORT OF THING EVEN HAPPEN?
IS THIS THE ONLY GUY WHO'S NOT ON THE LIST?
A
"A"...?
INAGA
A
KAGESA
TACHIB
IT'S SAKURA. DID SOMETHING HAPPEN?
BEEP
MESSAGE RECEIVED FROM SAKURA:
THIS IS SAKURA. THERE'S SOMETHING I FORGOT TO MENTION EARLIER...
"THERE'S SOMETHING I FORGOT TO MENTION EARLIER. ABOUT ODAGIRI'S BODY."
WHIRL
...

DRIP
"MAKE SURE YOU DISPOSE OF IT PROPERLY."
DRIP
...
CLENCH
SOMETHING URGENT CAME UP. I'M GOING TO HAVE TO STEP AWAY FOR A BIT.
FOCUS ON GATHERING INFORMATION UNTIL I GET BACK.
WHA— WAIT A SECOND!
SQUIRM あわ
YOU'RE LEAVING ME ALONE AT A TIME LIKE THIS?!
あわ SQUIRM

YOU OKAY? YER NOT LOOKING TOO GOOD THERE.
UH... YEAH! I'M FINE!
HA HA
はは、
I THINK EVERYTHING IS HITTING ME ALL AT ONCE. IT'S A LOT.
WELL, WE GOT THAT GENERATOR GOING AGAIN, SO I'M SURE WE'LL BE SEEING *THAT GUY* SOON.
THEN WE CAN GET A BITE TO EAT AND REST FOR A LITTLE BIT.
WE'LL HAVE ONE PERSON FROM EACH GROUP GO AND PASS OUT THE FOOD, AS USUAL.
YOU ALL ARE OKAY WITH THAT, RIGHT?
NOD
コク

...
IF WE ARRANGE WHO'S IN CHARGE OF FOOD JUST RIGHT, YOU'LL HAVE A CHANCE TO TALK WITH YOUR FRIEND FREELY.
WHISPER
PAT
JUST HANG IN THERE A LITTLE LONGER.
MINAGAWA...
DON'T GET THE WRONG IDEA. YOU'RE THE ONLY ONE HERE WE'RE SURE IS INNOCENT. I JUST WANT TO MAKE SURE YOU OWE ME ONE LATER.
HMPH
THAT'S IT.
OKAY.

SO, ANYWAY, WHAT'S THIS OTHER PERSON LIKE?
BEATS ME. I DON'T EVEN KNOW HIS NAME.
ガチャ
KER-CHAK
HE NEVER TRIES TO GET IN CONTACT WITH ANYONE, SO I HAVE NO IDEA WHAT HE'S THINKING.
I... KNOW HIS SECRET.
クスッ
HEHEH
WHAT SECRET, YUKIMURA?
I HEARD HIM TALKING TO HIMSELF YESTERDAY WHEN I WAS SERVING THE FOOD.

AH! SO THIS IS WHERE HE WAS.
UM... EXCUSE ME?
SHAKE
THIS TIME I'LL MAKE IT OUT OF HERE FOR SURE.
MUTTER
I WON'T MAKE THE SAME MISTAKE I DID LAST TIME.
GRUMBLE
GRUMBLE

I'LL DEFINITELY BEAT *THIS* DEATH GAME!

Chapter 10

RATTLE
CLATTER
HEY, WHAT'S UP? IF YOU NEED SOMETHING CLEANED UP, YOU'RE BETTER OFF WAITING FOR THE CUSTODIAL CREW.
ODAGIRI TOLD ME THIS WAS PART OF MY "TRAINING" AS A NEW HIRE.
HA HA... THAT'S SO LIKE HIM. WELL, GOOD LUCK WITH YOUR "TRAINING".
PHEW
HEY, WAIT A SEC.
ERK

Y-YEAH? IS SOMETHING WRONG?
IT'S THAT LINEN CART.
THAT'S ONE THAT THE PREVIOUS CLEANING COMPANY USED. THEY'VE PROBABLY SWITCHED IT UP SINCE THEN.
!
IF THEY GIVE YOU ANY TROUBLE ABOUT BRINGING IT IN, TRY CALLING THE GENERAL AFFAIRS DIVISION. THEY SHOULD BE ABLE TO SORT IT OUT.

THANKS A LOT.
SIGH
ハア
THAT WAS TOO CLOSE FOR COMFORT. I THOUGHT FOR SURE SHE WAS ONTO ME.
I'M TRYING TO DO WHAT SAKURA SUGGESTED...
BUT IT STILL FEELS LIKE I'M GOING OUT ON A LIMB HERE.
IF I GET FOUND OUT, SHIT IS REALLY GONNA HIT THE FAN.

Chapter 10

ガラ
RATTLE
ガラ
CLATTER
GOOD, THEY'RE NOT HERE YET.
...
"THE CLEANING COMPANY", HUH?
THEY JUST HAPPEN TO BE CLEANERS WHO SPECIALIZE IN GETTING RID OF DEAD BODIES.
SAKURA SAID HE HAS A CONNECTION WITH THEM, SO NO ONE WOULD FIND OUT ABOUT ODAGIRI...
BUT WHY DOES HE HAVE A PERSONAL CONNECTION WITH A COMPANY LIKE THAT IN THE FIRST PLACE?

RUMBLE
IS THAT THEM?
SCREECH
ARE THEY FROM THE DISPOSAL CREW?
GULP
KER-CHAK

REACH
CREAK
UM... ARE YOU FROM THE CLEANING COMPANY WE'RE CONTRACTED WITH?
...
RATTLE
CLATTER
H-HEY, WAIT A MINUTE!
DON'T JUST HAUL IT OFF WITHOUT SAYING ANYTHING!
LUNGE
ARE YOU *REALLY* THE CLEANER I'VE BEEN WAITING AROUND FOR?

URNGH...
CLUNK
ACK!
WH-WHAT THE HELL HAPPENED TO YOU?
GRANGH!
URGGH!

AAANGH!
ビクッ
SHOCK
ANGGH!
URGGH...
...
ガラ
RATTLE
...
ガラ
CLATTER

WHA–?
KER-CHAK
KER-CHAK
CLATTER
CLATTER
WHAT'S UP WITH THIS GUY?
THIS IS THE GUY SAKURA HAS A CONNECTION TO?
GRAAGH
JUST WHO IS HE ANYWAY?
TCHK

ブルル…
RUMBLE
...
2
C1
BEEP BEEP BEEP
SAKURA
REMIND ME
MESSAGE
DECLINE
ACCEPT
SAKURA'S CALLING?
YEAH? THIS IS MIYAUCHI.
IT LOOKS LIKE THE HANDOFF OF YOUR "BAGGAGE" WENT WELL.
I'VE PUT IN FOR A FEW DAYS OF VACATION TIME FOR ODAGIRI. TRY TO RELAX. THINGS WILL BE FINE.

I TOLD THEM IT WAS TO SPEND TIME WITH HIS FAMILY, AND IT WENT OFF WITHOUT A HITCH.
HIS FAMILY?
ははっ HA HA
OH, DIDN'T YOU KNOW HE WAS MARRIED?
HE HAD A DAUGHTER IN HIGH SCHOOL. HE WAS ALWAYS SHOWING HER PICTURE AROUND. HE WAS VERY PROUD OF HER.
...
SACRIFICES MUST BE MADE IF YOU WANT TO GET THINGS DONE...
ESPECIALLY IF YOU'RE TRYING TO PROTECT SOMEONE IMPORTANT TO YOU.
LET ME KNOW IF YOU RUN INTO ANY MORE TROUBLE.
GOOD LUCK!

BEEP
UM... SAKURA—!
IS IT WORK? YOU MUST BE VERY BUSY.
SO SORRY TO INTERRUPT OUR MEAL.
MY SUPERVISOR WENT ON FAMILY LEAVE, SO I HAD TO MAKE SOME SPECIAL AR-RANGEMENTS.
HA HA. HE'S LUCKY TO HAVE SOMEONE HE CAN DEPEND ON.
AND SINCE YOU'RE SO DEPENDABLE, SAKURA, THERE'S SOMETHING I'D LIKE TO ASK YOU.
OH, IS THAT WHY YOU ASKED ME HERE TODAY...
GENTO WEEKLY
EDITOR-IN-CHIEF
TETSUYA KUBO
MR. EDITOR-IN-CHIEF?

YES, INDEED.
BLINK
ピクッ
I'D LIKE TO ASK ABOUT A GIRL NAMED SHINZAKI WHO WORKED AT YOUR COMPANY.
OH, YEAH?

COFFEE
Original Blend since 1961
SALMON
NOW I CAN FOCUS ON KYO.
はぁ
SIGH
I CAN'T LET MYSELF GET DISCOURAGED.
ぱく
MUNCH
!
LOOKS LIKE THE LIGHTS STILL AREN'T ON AROUND HERE.
STEP
JUST BECAUSE WE GOT ACCESS TO THE NEXT FLOOR DOESN'T MEAN THAT THE ELECTRICITY HAS COME BACK EVERYWHERE.
SO THEY'VE ALREADY FINISHED EATING AND MOVED ON TO THE NEXT FLOOR.

YEAH. THIS WHOLE "GET THE POWER BACK ON" TASK IS TRICKIER THAN IT SEEMS.
EVEN IF WE FIND THE DOOR TO THE NEXT FLOOR, THAT DOESN'T MEAN WE CAN GO THROUGH.
KNOCK
WE HAVE TO FIND THE GENERATORS THAT ARE STILL SHUT DOWN AND GET THEM GOING AGAIN.
WE NEED TO KNOW WHERE THE FOOD AND THE BATHROOMS ARE. THAT'S WHY WE HAVE TO MAKE A CAREFUL SEARCH WHENEVER WE'RE LOOKING THROUGH A ROOM.
MAN, SCREW THEM FOR MAKING US GO THROUGH ALL THIS ANNOYING BULLSHIT.
HMPH
UMM...

CAN'T WE JUST HAVE THE KILLERS TELL US WHO THEY ARE SO WE CAN ALL WORK TOGETHER AND GET OUT OF HERE?
!
THEN THERE'D BE NO NEED FOR US TO TRY AND KILL EACH OTHER.
WE COULD SAVE EVERYONE!
STEP
SUPPOSEDLY THAT'S NOT AN OPTION.
AT LEAST THAT'S WHAT THIS ONE GUY SAID. BUT HE WAS ONE OF THE KILLERS, AND HE DIED BECAUSE HE REVEALED HIMSELF.

DON'T YOU SEE? WE *WANT* TO BE HERE!
IF WE KILL ALL OF YOU PLAYERS, OUR WISHES WILL BE GRANTED!
CLICK
カチャ

CLENCH
DOES THAT MEAN THAT KILLERS MADE A BARGAIN, JUST LIKE ME?
!
SO, THAT'S THE KIND OF BARGAIN THEY MADE.
THERE'S NO WAY THE KILLERS WILL STOP TRYING TO GO AFTER THE PLAYERS.
WE'LL NEVER GET EVERYONE TO WORK TOGETHER TO ESCAPE.
SQUEAK
CLENCH
THE GUY WHO CAME UP WITH THIS GAME KEEPS COMING UP WITH MORE AND MORE FUCKED UP SHIT.

SIGH
EVENTUALLY HE STARTED FIRING OFF RANDOM SHOTS.
A BUNCH OF PEOPLE GOT GRAZED WHILE RUNNING AWAY, BUT IF THEY HID, THEY JUST ENDED UP DYING.
ANOTHER GUY WENT TO GO TURN ON A GENERATOR BY HIMSELF AND GOT ELECTROCUTED.
AFTER THAT, WE STARTED GOING AROUND IN GROUPS OF 3 OR MORE TO AVOID GETTING JUMPED BY ONE OF THE KILLERS.
WELL, EXCEPT FOR THAT ONE GUY.
...
SO THAT'S WHY YER IDEA WON'T WORK.
WE DON'T HAVE ANY CHOICE BUT TO FOLLOW THE PLAN OF WHICHEVER SICK FUCK IS RUNNING THIS THING.

HMPH
チッ
SO, THE "KILLERS" ARE TRYING TO KILL ALL THE "PLAYERS"...
AND THE "PLAYERS" ARE PLANNING THEIR ESCAPE, SO THEY CAN AVOID BEING MURDERED BY THE "KILLERS."
LOOKS LIKE THAT'S THE KIND OF DEATH GAME THIS IS.
WHAT IS IT, MINAGAWA?
BE CAREFUL.
HUH?
YOU'RE THE ONLY ONE WE DEFINITELY KNOW ISN'T A KILLER, SO YOU'RE KIND OF A KEY PERSON IN THIS.

BUT ON THE OTHER HAND, FROM THE KILLERS' POINT OF VIEW, YOU'RE A LIABILITY THAT THEY DEFINITELY WANT TO TAKE OUT.
THAT'S RIGHT.
CREAK
IF IT COMES DOWN TO JUST TWO PEOPLE IN THE END...
IF YOU'RE ONE OF THEM, THE OTHER PLAYER CAN RELAX AND FOCUS ON ESCAPING.
IN OTHER WORDS...

THE ACTIONS YOU TAKE...
CAN RADICALLY ALTER THE BALANCE OF THIS DEATH GAME.
GASP

YOU'RE THE ONE THAT THE KILLERS WILL BE GUNNING FOR FIRST.

EDC COLLECTION 4
PROJECT SURVIVAL (WORKING TITLE)

THIS ONLINE COMPETITIVE SURVIVAL GAME FOR 16 PLAYERS IS CURRENTLY UNDER DEVELOPMENT BY EDC. THE PLAYERS CANNOT ESCAPE THEIR CONFINEMENT WITHOUT EACH OTHER'S HELP. HOWEVER, THEIR EFFORTS AT COOPERATION ARE HAMPERED BY THE FACT THAT SOME OF THEIR NUMBER ARE SECRETLY KILLERS TRYING TO PICK OFF THE REST OF THE PLAYERS ONE BY ONE. PROJECT SURVIVAL IS CURRENTLY BEING PLAYTESTED.

THERE ARE WEAPONS HIDDEN ON EACH FLOOR, JUST LIKE KINJO WAS SAYING BEFORE.
I KNOW WHERE THEY ARE, SO TAKE THE OPPORTUNITY TO GET THEM WHEN YOU CAN.
NOD
I DON'T KNOW WHAT'S IN EACH CACHE THOUGH, SO WHATEVER YOU FIND THERE IS JUST THE LUCK OF THE DRAW.
EVEN SO, IT SHOULD BE SOMETHING USEFUL.
THEY'LL GET SUSPICIOUS IF YOU SPEND TOO MUCH TIME IN THE BATHROOM, SO I'LL EXPLAIN QUICKLY.

TRY TO REMEMBER AS MUCH AS YOU CAN.
HEH クスッ
YOU SURE ARE WORRIED ABOUT ME, AREN'T YOU?
HUH?
I WAS JUST THINKING YOU SEEMED LIKE A VERY KIND PERSON.
THANKS FOR EVERYTHING.
...
NOT AT ALL.
I'M JUST DOING MY JOB.

YEAH, YOU'RE RIGHT. SORRY IF I WEIRDED YOU OUT.
I SHOULD FOCUS ON MY JOB TOO...
KYO, WHY *DID* YOU AGREE TO JOIN THIS DEATH GAME?
SO I CAN GET WHAT I'M LOOKING FOR.
BEEEP
WHO IS IT?

Chapter 11

SORRY TO PULL YOU AWAY FROM YOUR WORK...
BUT YOU REALLY NEED A BREAK, EVEN IF I HAVE TO DRAG YOU AWAY KICKING AND SCREAMING.
YOU HAVE TO REST *SOMETIME*, YOU KNOW.
STEP
SORRY ABOUT THAT.
I WAS JUST SURPRISED BECAUSE YOU SUDDENLY JOKED ABOUT ASKING ME OUT ON A DATE OR SOMETHING.
HEHEH!
YOU WANT ME TO... GO GET A CUP OF TEA WITH YOU?

SORRY, I'M IN THE MIDDLE OF SOMETHING RIGHT NOW.
THERE ARE A FEW THINGS I WANT TO ASK YOU ABOUT ODAGIRI.
GASP
はっ
SHIT! DID SHE FIND OUT THAT I KILLED HIM?
I DON'T KNOW WHAT HE WAS THINKING, GOING OUT ON LEAVE ALL OF A SUDDEN.

ハア
PHEW
SORRY THAT ODAGIRI JUST DUMPED EVERYTHING ON YOU.
IT LOOKS LIKE YOU CAN DO THE WORK THOUGH, SO IT SEEMS LIKE IT'S WORKING OUT.
OH...
YOU HAVE TO TAKE A BREATHER NOW AND THEN THOUGH, OR YOU WON'T BE ABLE TO KEEP IT UP.
WOULD YOU LET ME TAKE YOU OUT SOMEWHERE TO MAKE IT UP TO YOU...
AS A FAVOR TO YOUR SUPERVISOR?
SMILE
ニコッ
OKAY.

PHEW
I'M GLAD SHE DIDN'T FIND OUT ABOUT ODAGIRI.
OTHERWISE...
I'D HAVE TO FIGURE OUT HOW TO KILL HER NEXT.
GASP
WHAT THE HELL AM I THINKING?
...

KER-CHAK
WHAT IS THIS PLACE?
THERE'S A *GARDEN* INSIDE THE BUILDING?
IT'S ALL REAL, OF COURSE.
STEP
ALL THE DIFFERENT FLOWERS EVEN BLOOM IN THEIR PROPER SEASONS.

STEP
GO AHEAD, HAVE A SEAT.
WAIT A SECOND WHILE I BREW SOME TEA.
I'M HARDLY AN EXPERT, BUT I QUITE LIKE THIS BLEND.
CLACK
WHY IS THERE A PLACE LIKE THIS IN THE MIDDLE OF...?
POUR
HEHEH
DO YOU THINK SOMETHING A BIT MORE MURDER-ORIENTED WOULD BE A BETTER FIT FOR THE COMPANY?
...

ORIGINALLY, THE GARDEN WAS JUST A HOBBY FOR THE COMPANY PRESIDENT...
BUT NOW IT'S MORE OF A PRIVATE LOUNGE FOR THE EXECUTIVES.
THE EXECUTIVES?
OH, YOU'RE HERE ALREADY.
SQUEAK
AH, SIR! IF I HAD KNOWN YOU'D ARRIVED, I WOULD HAVE COME TO GET YOU.
PITTER
PATTER
DON'T BOTHER YOURSELF WITH THAT. YOU BROUGHT HIM HERE, AND THAT'S WHAT'S IMPORTANT.
...

AND YOU ARE?
ALLOW ME TO INTRODUCE MYSELF. I'M THE REPRESENTATIVE DIRECTOR OF EDC.
WHA—?!
CLATTER
I'VE HEARD ABOUT YOU FROM TANAHASHI, AND I WANTED TO TAKE THE TIME TO TALK TO YOU.

I BELIEVE I'LL HAVE A CUP OF TEA AS WELL. TANAHASHI, IF YOU PLEASE.
CERTAINLY. ONE MOMENT, SIR.
HA HA. COME NOW, YOU DON'T HAVE TO LOOK SO SCARED.
WHINE
OUTSTANDING PEOPLE ARE VALUABLE TO THE COMPANY. I WANTED TO SEE YOU FOR MYSELF.
AS YOU ALREADY KNOW, THOSE OF US WHO WEAR SUITS IN THIS COMPANY HAVE ALL EXPERIENCED DEATH GAMES FIRSTHAND.
Entertainment
WE'VE BEEN ABLE TO ACHIEVE EXCELLENT RESULTS AS A COMPANY...
BY LOOKING FOR CANDIDATES WITH THE EXPERIENCE AND FORCE OF WILL THAT COMES FROM SURVIVING A DEATH GAME.
WHINE

CLINK
カチャ
NOT EVERYONE IS AS EXCEPTIONAL AS TANAHASHI HERE OR SUZUKI.
THANK YOU, SIR.
HOWEVER, THAT DOESN'T MEAN THAT SUCH EMPLOYEES ARE ALWAYS ABLE TO WORK FOR A LONG TIME.
SOME LOSE THEIR COMPOSURE, OTHERS END UP OVERDOING THINGS. THERE ARE MANY KINDS OF PEOPLE, AFTER ALL.
THAT'S WHY I'D LIKE YOU TO APPLY YOURSELF TO YOUR WORK WITHOUT GETTING TOO WOUND UP OVER THINGS.
EXCUSE ME?

DON'T WORRY ABOUT THAT BUSINESS WITH ODAGIRI.
HUH?
WE KNOW ALL ABOUT WHAT YOU DID.
PUFF
THE FACT THAT YOU KILLED ODAGIRI AND THAT YOU USED AN OUTSIDE GROUP TO DISPOSE OF HIS CORPSE.
SHIT!
GRAB

HUSH NOW.
THE DIRECTOR IS IN THE MIDDLE OF TALKING.
PRESS
...
THERE'S SOMEONE YOU KNOW PARTICIPATING IN THE DEATH GAME THAT WE'RE CURRENTLY WORKING ON. YOU'VE BEEN GIVING THEM QUITE A BIT OF SUPPORT, HAVEN'T YOU?
...
YOU WERE WORRIED ABOUT LEAVING HER FATE IN ODAGIRI'S HANDS, SO YOU KILLED HIM... I SUPPOSE.
IT IS INDEED PROMISING TO SEE PEOPLE KILLING EACH OTHER OVER THE DIRECTION OF A GAME.
WHAT?

CLINK
カチャ
IF YOU WEREN'T SO ENGAGED... WELL THEN, YOU'D HARDLY BE A GOOD FIT FOR A MANAGEMENT TRACK POSITION, WOULD YOU?
YOU EVEN DID A GOOD JOB TAKING CARE OF THE BODY. I CAN'T WAIT TO SEE WHAT THE FUTURE HOLDS FOR YOU.
TWIST
ギリッ
IS THAT ALL YOU HAVE TO SAY WHEN ONE OF YOUR EMPLOYEES GETS KILLED?
IT WAS PRETTY PATHETIC FOR HIM TO BE KILLED SO EASILY BY HIS OWN TRAINEE.
SIGH
ハァ
UNFORTUNATELY, THAT'S ALL ODAGIRI WAS GOOD FOR.
IT WAS A MISTAKE TO PUT A GUY LIKE HIM IN CHARGE OF YOUR TRAINING.

HA HA. YOU'RE AS HARSH AS EVER, TANAHASHI, BUT THAT'S WHAT I LIKE ABOUT YOU.
WHAT'S WRONG WITH THESE PEOPLE?
THEY'RE ALL COMPLETELY FUCKING INSANE!
GULP
I DON'T CARE WHAT ANY OF YOU PEOPLE THINK...
AS LONG AS I CAN SAVE KYO.

I'LL DO WHATEVER I CAN TO GET HER OUT OF YOUR SHITTY DEATH GAME!
クス
AHEH!!,
AH HA HA HA HA!
YOU'RE GOING TO SAVE HER? *THAT* GIRL?

HA HA... NOW, NOW. WE MUSTN'T LAUGH AT MIYAUCHI. IT'S RUDE.
AHEM
I'M SO SORRY! I JUST COULDN'T HELP MYSELF!
HAVEN'T YOU HEARD WHY SHE'S AGREED TO JOIN THIS GAME?
NO, WHY?
IT LOOKS LIKE ODAGIRI WAS BEING A BIT MEAN-SPIRITED HIMSELF. PERHAPS WE WERE TOO QUICK TO WRITE HIM OFF.
HMM
MIYAUCHI...

YOU DON'T KNOW THE FIRST THING ABOUT THAT GIRL.
ピチャ
DRIP
OH, NO, NO, YUKIMURA. THAT'S NO GOOD.
DRIP
ピチャ
YOU SEE, AS SOON AS I'M ALONE WITH SOMEONE I CAN SHOW MY TRUE COLORS.
グリグリッ
TUG

HRRRK...?!

ACCCH...!
I'M THE ONE WHO'S GOING TO SURVIVE THIS DEATH GAME.
TIGHTEN

I'LL KILL EACH AND EVERY LAST ONE OF YOU.

SHE AGREED TO JOIN THIS DEATH GAME BECAUSE SHE WANTED SOMETHING THAT ONLY WE COULD PROVIDE.
OUR COMPANY MAY BE CRUEL, BUT WE ALWAYS KEEP OUR PROMISES.
IF SHE CAN MAKE IT THROUGH THIS DEATH GAME AND COME BACK ALIVE, WE WILL GIVE HER THAT WHICH SHE DESIRES.
WHAT WOULD YOU KNOW ABOUT WHAT SHE WANTS? YOU DON'T KNOW HER!
CLATTER
ガタッ
"I WANT YOU TO TELL ME ABOUT THE DEATH GAME WHERE MY SISTER DIED."

"I'M GOING TO FIND THE PERSON WHO KILLED HER AND AVENGE HER DEATH."
SHOCK
THAT IS HER DESIRE.
WHAT?
N-NO WAY!
CLENCH
MIYAUCHI...

...SHE AGREED TO TAKE PART IN THIS DEATH GAME SO SHE COULD KILL YOU.

TO BE CONTINUED...

TONOGAI

NOMURA
KAWANO
KOIDE
OOTUKA
ARAKAWA

KANDA

Dead Company, Volume 2

Manga by Yoshiki Tonogai

Editor - Lena Atanassova
Editorial Associate - Becca Grace
Translator - David Bove
Copy Editor - Tina Tseng
Retouching and Lettering - Vibrraant Publishing Studio
Cover Designer - Aracelli Ejarque Villegas

Graphic Designer - Sol DeLeo
Marketing Associate - Kae Winters
Digital Marketing Associate - Kitt Burgess
Digital Content Associate - Shraboni Dutta
Business Development Associate - Marissa Galiley
Licensing Associate - Julia Stasio
COO & Publisher - Marc Visnick
Founder - Stu Levy

A TOKYOPOP® Manga

TOKYOPOP Inc.
4136 Del Rey Ave., Suite 502
Marina del Rey, CA 90292-5604

E-mail: info@TOKYOPOP.com
Come visit us online at www.TOKYOPOP.com

www.facebook.com/TOKYOPOP
www.twitter.com/TOKYOPOP
www.instagram.com/TOKYOPOP

ISBN: 978-1-4278-7409-2

First TOKYOPOP Printing: November 2023

Printed in CANADA

STOP
THIS IS THE BACK OF THE BOOK!
How do you read manga-style? It's simple!
Let's practice — just start in the top right
panel and follow the numbers below!
1
2
3
4
5
6
7
8
9
10
READ
RIGHT
-TO-
LEFT